IN EXTREMIS

A HELLBOUND NOVELLA

DAVID MCCAFFREY

Britain's Next
BESTSELLER

First published in 2015 by 6e Publishing
This edition published by:
Britain's Next Bestseller
An imprint of Live It Ventures LTD
27 Old Gloucester Road
London.
WC1N 3AX
www.bnbsbooks.co.uk
Copyright © 2018 by David McCaffrey

All enquiries should be addressed to Britain's Next Bestseller.
@BNBSbooks
www.davidmccaffrey.net
ISBN 978-1-910565-81-0
Cover designed by Rowland Kell

For Mary Ann Nicols, Annie Chapman, Elizabeth Stride, Catherine Eddowes and Mary Jane Kelly –
let history never forget your names

Brethren
   NOUN
   plural noun: **brethren**

Fellow Christians or members of a male religious order.
See also brother.

Synonyms: believers · communicants · adherents · followers
loyal followers · loyal members · congregation · brethren
flock · people belonging to a particular group. community ·
company · group · body · mass · throng assembly · Church ·
church membership parishioners · churchgoers

"One day men will look back and say I gave birth to the twentieth century."
From Hell

SHE REMINDS ME OF THE WHORE.

The fireplace glowed softly. Its deep ambers, reds and livid purples embossed the melted kettle hanging on a hook above it, in a shifting kaleidoscope of colour. Its flickering incandescence painted the room in shifting shadow, adding depth to the small and cluttered reality. A bedside table, cupboard, and chair encapsulated its furnishings. Alongside the stack of neatly folded clothes on the chair was skin and muscle from her abdomen and thighs.

Thought they belonged there.

The body on the bed was barely recognisable as a human being, never mind that of a woman. Her legs were splayed apart, the right thigh shorn of skin and the left stripped down to the muscle that now occupied the chair.

The face had been utterly destroyed – cheeks, eyebrows, nose and ears, all removed. Her lips were blanched with an incision running down to her chin. The cut to her neck was so deep, the ivory white of her spine could be seen.

Having had time to indulge, he had positioned her right arm on the mattress, forearm facing upwards. Her fist was clenched tightly, as though holding a secret object. Her left arm had been placed across the cavity that was once her abdomen, with the gaping maw now resembling a Christmas present ripped open by an impatient child. Both her arms were covered in jagged lacerations that could only be described as defensive cuts.

He had kissed her breasts for a while after their removal, savouring the sweet taste of blood. Then he placed one of them beneath her head, like a deflated pillow, alongside her uterus and kidneys. The other was placed under her right foot, alongside her liver. After positioning her intestines down the right-hand side of her body and her spleen to the left, he had carefully removed her heart, wrapping it in cloth and placing it in his bag. Eddowes' ears he had clipped and taken just for jolly, but Kelly's heart meant something more. It showed he was reaching the antithesis of his crusade. Daubing the wall with his wife's initials had been his final act, a subtle clue for the police to deliberate.

It hadn't taken much persuasion for him to be invited to her room. His original intent had been to take her down one of the alleyways as he had the others. Knowing that whatever God existed in heaven could see him had always been exhilarating, and upon seeing her he had immediately craved the sensation once again. But with her invite, he had realised that in the privacy of her dwellings there was no obligation for him to hurry. He would have all the time he needed to create his masterpiece with little risk of discovery, unlike Stride.

That idiot salesman, Diemschutz, had almost stepped on him, forcing him to seek out another to sate his desires that night. Encountering Eddowes had been good fortune.

But even then, he had felt rushed, knowing that Mitre Square would soon resonate with the thrum of people. Working in the comfort and safety of Kelly's modest residence, the glow from the fireplace had made him feel more powerful than ever, almost messianic. Tonight he had been able to work methodically he had yearned for, and it pleased him.

Carefully folding down his sleeves, he retrieved his coat from the back of the chair and pulled it on, fastening it tight over his blood-soaked shirt and waistcoat. Recovering some leather gloves from the pockets, he pulled them on slowly, flattening them down between the webs of his fingers.

Should he be stopped, no explanation would justify his sanguinary appearance, but from a distance, he would simply resemble a doctor making a late night house call or a shabby man from Battersea passing muster as one of the respectable poor. Not distinct enough to have locals reach for Keating's bug powder, but unfortunate enough in appearance to ensure he could hide in plain sight. And if he left now, the likelihood of him encountering a policeman on his way back to his lodgings would be slim.

Throwing the girl's bloody clothing into the fire's dying embers, he placed the knife back into the bag and snapped it shut before moving towards the door. Casting a look back towards the bed, he caught sight of his face in the mirror on the opposite wall. It was an image familiar and yet, at the same time, alien to him. Sweat had matted his brown hair to his head, his face visibly flushed even in the soft firelight. His moustache remained perfectly groomed, its semblance of normalcy darkly amusing amongst the scene of abhorrence around him.

It was the face of a husband, father, and now... a monster.

The man I have become was not the man I was born.

Shaking sentiment aside, he left the room and locked the door behind him, placing the key back in his pocket. Casually, James Maybrick turned out of Millers Court and made his way up towards Middlesex Street. Gas lamps lit his way, the air thick with the smell of gasoline and sulphur.

Christ Church spire rose up in the distance as he moved between the vendors setting up their stalls. The few horse-drawn carriages negated the cobbled streets fraught with manure. He gazed at the whores making their way to their lodgings with their night's earnings, their presence representing the epitome of London's human refuse. It was as though its poorest were pulling themselves up from the very ground around him, with the hardship of existing in such times etched upon their faces.

He was distracted by a brief surge of adrenaline as he remembered the girl's blood-soaked body. Flesh separated and puckered, he had left her in such a manner that her sacrification would be remembered.

The recollection aroused him. Death and sensuality combined to create a unique vision of purity and abhorrence. Though he had experienced doubts since the beginning, he knew the mission he had been tasked with was necessary. It had given him a purity of purpose. These women needed to be punished, all in her name. And yet he felt guilt. Not enough to consume him, but enough to have it niggling away in the back of his mind like a parasite infecting his very soul.

May God forgive me for the deeds I committed on Kelly, no heart no heart.

Reaching Middlesex Street, he climbed the steps to his lodgings and unlocked the weather-beaten door. The gloom that enveloped him permeated his clothing and chilled his bones.

The coming dawn made it possible for him to see enough to place his bag on the bedside table and climb onto the bed. His procedures always left him feeling drained, both physically and mentally, but this time it was more. He felt feverish, uncertain as to whether it was due to the remnants of adrenaline in his body or arsenic withdrawal. His loss of focus ensured he didn't notice the man sitting in the corner of the room.

"I fear you might have become a problem, James," the man announced. "The latitude once provided you has come to an end with this latest demonstration."

Startled, Maybrick lunged for a knife from his bag but realising who the intruder was settled back on the edge of the bed.

"I thought it had been agreed there would be no direct contact. Your stipulation, Quinn, not mine."

"That was true, but you've gone too far this evening," he chided.

"You've seen her?" Maybrick queried.

Even in shadow, he saw Quinn nodding. "She should have done something about that broken window," he mocked, slowly moving forwards into the dim light.

Though older than Maybrick, Quinn remained lean and rugged from his military days. His dark hair was cropped close to his head, accenting his shallow brow and aquiline nose. "I do believe you will have cemented your legend with Kelly. But she is the last, so the question you must now ask yourself is whether you wish that legend to be infinite or simply transitory?"

Maybrick quickly stood and closed the distance

between him and Quinn. "And who are you to tell me I am finished?" Veins throbbed in his neck as he leaned menacingly closer. "Remember you came to me, requesting to be part of my mission."

Quinn snorted a laugh, seeming to sense his perturbation. "Mission? I think you have an overinflated opinion of your actions. You are correct, we did approach you. Your work has made you singularly unique, in London if not the world. Soon, all will know your name and what you have done here. But do not ever think that you have the choice of autonomy. We came to you, but now you belong to us. This Kelly business has crossed a line that cannot be erased. If you are caught… well, I don't imagine I need to advise you of what will happen if you are arrested."

"And what makes you think they will catch me?" Maybrick said, with a tight-lipped smile. "They have no idea who I am. And with Warren in charge, I can't imagine they will ever come close. The man is incompetent."

"Incompetent he may be," Quinn replied. "But Abberline is far from so. He will make a connection. If he finds you, he finds us. That cannot happen."

He moved away from Quinn and towards the window. The dawn was casting its soft light over the cobbled streets, making even Whitechapel look enticing.

"What do you want from me?" he asked quietly.

"This world disappoints you, does it not?" Quinn asked. "Your crusade was intended to create something exceptional, exquisite even. But you have become lost amongst your own desires, my friend. What you are doing no longer falls under the rubric of surgery… you work in darker hues. Kelly must be the last. Any more and the East End of London will explode. We already have Lusk and his Vigilante Committee roaming the streets, accosting every fletcher, leather apron and anyone trading with a knife. Warren is poised to retire, people are afraid. What you have accomplished cannot be understated. We have large plans for this city, and our vision of social reform has been led by you… you should be proud. But the increased enthusiasm for your work threatens to undermine those plans. You are upsetting the status quo, for want of a better word."

"I think you should leave," Maybrick responded, without turning around. He could feel the anger swelling inside him. Quinn's demands were an insult to his integrity and all he had done for them.

"Very well," Quinn said, opening the door and standing in the hallway. "But pay heed, James. If you choose to ignore my advice, the consequences will be severe. The men you have chosen to ally yourself with will not take insubordination lightly. Your legacy is secured for the next hundred years, but only if it remains shrouded in mystery. Discovery of who you really are will only be consigning you to history as another sick malcontent."

He heard the door click shut but continued to look out of the window, his sense of swelling anger tempered with anxiety. Could Quinn be right? Had he gone too far with Kelly? While with her, it had felt only right that she be his masterpiece, the one representing a facsimile of his fevered dreams. But what if in his fugue state, he had left some piece of evidence that could be traced back to him? A more significant concern, though he wouldn't have admitted it to Quinn, was if he had left something that led back to them.

As he watched the sun rise higher in the sky towards Spitalfields, he realised he needed some distance from London and his indulgences. At least in Liverpool with Bunny and the children he would have space to consider his next move. However, Maybrick knew even Merseyside wasn't far enough away that Quinn and his employers couldn't reach him.

He was beginning to wonder if there was anywhere in the world The Brethren couldn't find him.

"In the pursuit of my holy cause, I… did things. Terrible things. Unspeakable things. The world condemned me, but it didn't matter because I believed I was right and the world was wrong. I believed I was the divine messenger. I believed I was…"

Comes The Inquisitor

THE DIMLY LIT ROOM HAD AN AIR OF AUTHORITY ABOUT IT, Quinn considered, taking his seat around the large oval table amongst the other members.

With the medieval tapestries adorning the walls, the dark mahogany woodwork and the thick green carpet, he realised the room was meant to project order and history. Having them sit around a table together was a nice touch too. Sebastian Archard, residing president of The Brethren Organisation, could then see all of their faces at once.

Politicians, police officers, solicitors, and surgeons, they met in secret every month where they would share success stories, enjoy debaucheries of expensive wine and exotic food, and revel in their positions as masters of their own universes. Always a different location, always a different time, Archard had formed The Brethren because he believed many individuals shared his singular view on society, that it was broken and that they alone could make it better.

Slowly gaining numbers and, by default power, they had been an oligarchy in London long before Quinn joined them. From the Chartist Movement in 1839 to the repeal of the Corn Laws in 1846, they had exercised an undemocratic agenda serving their own interests. Building their numbers with likeminded individuals who had the power to change things, they had subtly been laying the groundwork for a larger plan. A plan only Archard knew for sure.

Holding no position in the upper echelons of society would have usually precluded someone of Quinn's low social class gaining entry to the organisation's inner circle.

Nevertheless, having a detailed knowledge of the East End of London, and his time with the 1st Battalion of the 18th Irish Regiment had convinced them he had enough of a résumé to act as a go-between for them and the people of Whitechapel. The infrastructure of poverty made them a society, unlike anything The Brethren's upper-class clientele had encountered. However, although they despised it, they had to admit that they needed a liaison to the people currently suffering at the hands of their vanity project for their plans to be successful.

As though on cue, their ostentatious president swept into the room through the large double doors at the rear of the room and moved around to take his seat at the head of the table. His appearance always reminded Quinn of an undertaker – black suit and tie, white shirt and slicked-back hair. Archard slowly made eye contact with every one of the twelve members, holding each man's gaze just long enough for it to be considered uncomfortable. He paused upon reaching Quinn, making no effort to hide his disdain at having to tolerate a working-class presence in his sanctuary.

"So?" he asked forcefully. "What news on Maybrick? Has he agreed to our terms?"

"I am unable to confirm that at present, but I delivered

your proposal as requested. I have also initiated contact with his wife. If he refuses to acquiesce to our demands, I will see to it the situation is dealt with."

"Ensure it is, Mr Quinn," Archard said curtly. "The attention his latest crime will generate is unacceptable. He has become nothing more than an educated version of Lusk and his vigilantes.

If he refuses to abstain from this deluded mission of his voluntarily, you will ensure he does so forcefully… and permanently."

Quinn nodded his understanding. Quinn's initiative in meeting with Maybrick's wife had been met with an acknowledgement he had been seeking since being accepted into their organisation.

He remained relieved The Brethren were yet to realise the purpose behind his eager desire to join their ranks, but also knew that if they were to discover his deception, disposing of him would be a relatively easy task. Therefore, he would remain careful as to his motive for gaining Florence Maybrick's confidence. He needed her to ensure his plan for her husband's punishment would be achievable. By disposing of Maybrick, he would not only appease his own sense of justice but would take care of someone who was potentially becoming a problem for them.

The man who had proclaimed himself Jack the Ripper had to die.

"Don't mind me giving the trade name. Wasn't good enough to post this before I got all the red ink off my hands. Curse it. No luck yet. They say I'm a doctor now. Ha ha."
Dear Boss Letter

13TH NOVEMBER, 1888
BATTLECREASE HOUSE, AIGBURTH, LIVERPOOL

FLORENCE SMILED AT THE CHILDREN AS THEY CHASED EACH other around the living room.

James and Gladys had been excitable since they received word their father was on his way home. James especially loved the nickname his father had for him, Bobo, and would giggle every time he heard it. She wished she could feel the same about his coming back, but knew all too well that upon his return home, he would find some reason to beat her.

Florence wished she could hate him, but though she had tried so hard over the years, she could never wholly bring herself to despise her husband truly. It had little to do with him being the father of her children, and more because she knew he was a man at war with himself. His addiction to arsenic did little to help his violent temperament. But after contracting malaria in Norfolk, Virginia, while working there, and with quinine being unsuccessful as a treatment, it had become something of a panacea as far as he was concerned.

With her gold ringlets and huge violet eyes, the twenty-six-year-old chatelaine, known as Florie to her friends, was considered the most beautiful woman in Liverpool, an accolade she was aware of but gave little credence to. It would have been easy to be swept along in the wake of such attention, especially considering her Alabama upbringing where being flirtatious was considered part of a Southern woman's genetic makeup. But her marriage to James had ensured that any attention such a bestowment would bring her was neutered. He was fiercely protective of her. His violent tendencies were only an extension of his jealousy and paranoia. Were he to learn of Alfred, he would surely kill her. Despite the women Florie knew he courted behind her back, his hypocrisy would be evident if he learned of his existence.

Her life seemed so far away from the one she had envisioned since she'd met James on the SS Baltic on her journey from America to Liverpool. He had seemed the perfect combination of the mature father figure she had craved all her life and a worldly self-assured man with a taste for dangerous living. Her mother, however, Baroness Caroline von Roques, had never liked James. She had thought him too old at forty-one, besides being crude and abrasive. But Florie had found him charming and a direct contrast to Southern men, with their false charm and loquacious drawl.

Florie's thoughts drifted towards her gentleman visitor from last week. Thomas Quinn had undoubtedly made an impression upon her. His well-dressed and statuesque demeanour had been in direct contrast with his cockney dialect. His unexpected visit had been under the pretence that he knew James from a previous business partnership. This was something she was unaware of, but admittedly knew little of her husband's activities. Staying only a short time, Thomas had said he would return this week to speak with her again, hoping to be able to provide her with more details as to a proposition. She had to admit she was intrigued, if not a little uneasy. His visit had seemed a little misleading, leaving her with the impression that there was more to his proposal that he had let on. She just couldn't put her finger on what was strange about his attention. That said businessmen rarely wished to deal with her, understandably, often choosing to deal with her more experienced husband. So Florie couldn't deny the fact that his wishing to speak with her had filled her with a sense of achievement, as though she was finally becoming accepted into British society.

With such emotions coursing through her, her mind couldn't help but shift towards thoughts of Alfred. Her lover for over a year, he was kind and generous. She had once seen these qualities in James, but they had now been diminished, in no small part to his addiction to arsenic. Her husband's hypochondria and gloomy disposition had become tiring of late, making time with Alfred all the more desirable. He was all that kept her from feeling lost. Married to a man she no longer loved, unable to see any way out, she hoped Alfred could save her. The way poets promised that lovers should.

And yet, she couldn't shake the feeling that an epoch was coming, and more importantly, that her husband would play a significant part in it.

The children running into her arms did little to sway her sense of foreboding.

"Yes, and why is that, Chief Superintendent? Mary Nicholls was a shilling whore. She wasn't killed for money, she didn't have any, her neighbours don't remember any enemies, and according to the doctor, she wasn't even sexually assaulted, yet somebody tore her to pieces in the streets!"

Jack the Ripper

MAYBRICK ROSE QUICKLY FROM THE BED AND RACED TO THE
bathroom, vomit splashing the floor beside the toilet.

When the retching ceased, he slumped onto his back
and gazed at the ceiling, subconsciously rubbing his
bruised knuckles. He remembered striking Florence upon
seeing her – the reason for it momentarily eluding him in
his delirium, like a snake evading capture. Slowly the
memory began to coalesce… Quinn.

The journey from London to Liverpool had been
uneventful and mundane, with only the transitory
excitement of reading about his own exploits in The Star
providing some respite. Bobo and Gladys had raced to see
him the moment he had stepped through the door,
wrapping themselves around his legs and asking if he had
gifts for them. A few minutes had been all he had given
them before turning his attention to Florence. Beautiful as
always, he had embraced her, once again realising how
fortunate he was to be married to such a prize,
simultaneously feeling guilt at what he had done. She'd

informed him about entertaining a gentleman going by the name of Quinn, which had only served to spoil the moment.

Anger had burst from him, and he'd delivered a flurry of blows to Florence's face. He had kissed her immediately after, caressing the swelling areas with tears in his eyes. He found his sorrow full and palpable, extremes in contradiction to his rage. In those moments, he felt like a hurricane, going from nothing to something powerful enough to destroy the environment surrounding him. At first, he had only felt it with the whores, but now it followed him wherever he went.

Taunting him to kill another one.

He apologised to Florence, knowing his behaviour had been from the realisation that The Brethren had been consorting with his wife. Though their motive was unclear, their representation in his home had forced him to comprehend that his time was running out. They would only have made themselves known here for one reason… to reinforce Quinn's warning that Kelly was the last.

Leaving Florie, he had retreated to his study and secured the arsenic from the bureau drawer. Quickly mixing the white powder, he had drunk it swiftly before it had finished dissolving in the glass. It was always the same; the anxiety of what he knew would follow. Horrific stomach cramps, nausea, vomiting. But it was worth it for what else it made him feel – strong and purified. Cleansed by way of suffering. The same as the whores in that respect – they achieved purification through his divine mission.

The nausea abating, Maybrick pulled himself up from beside the toilet and stared at himself in the mirror. His eyes were sunken, his skin alabaster to the point of being almost translucent. He staggered into the bedroom and collapsed onto the bed, writhing about as he pulled the sheets around his body.

Almost instantly, he slipped into a fevered sleep, dreams punctuating bouts of alertness and more waves of nausea. Torn flesh enticed him, glistening. He felt besieged by the multiple women beckoning him, willing his knife and their bodies to become one. Each pealing vision was revelatory, showing him a world filled with the desires he craved. His mind momentarily lost solidarity with every revelation. Then they would cry out to him for mercy, begging him to spare them. His mind became a war zone, the battle raging on for his very soul.

For the first time in years, he found himself praying.

I do not have the courage to take my own life. I believe I will tell her all, ask her to forgive me as I have forgiven her. I pray to god she will understand what she has done to me. Tonight I will pray for the women I have slaughtered.

"It's catching isn't it, violence."
Time After Time

SEBASTIAN ARCHARD SIGHED AS HE LEANED BACK INTO THE leather chair, rubbing his hands vigorously over his face as though to wake himself from sleep.

He picked up the folder and flicked it open, newspaper clippings, police reports, and crude witness drawings of the Whitechapel murderer unfurling in front of him. He studied each of them intently, his careful scrutiny of them causing the man before him to shift uncomfortably – the oppressive silence broken only by the tick of the clock, quietly sounding the passing seconds. Edwin Duggan tried to alleviate his anxiety by glancing around the office. The opulence of the décor was only offset by the subtlety of the paintwork, lending the room a welcoming feel that was bolstered by the fire crackling in the background. Yet he still felt cold, as though the intensity of Archard's presence was sucking the warmth from the very air.

Archard looked up at Duggan and carefully folded his glasses, placing them on the desk. He stared at him for a few beats before speaking.

"So, tell me why you think Maybrick is a bigger problem than I realise."

Duggan shifted through half a dozen responses before he settled on a suitable one. "Well, sir, you know we took Maybrick into our charge following his return from America. While there, we firmly believe that he was responsible for the eight murders which took place in Austin, Texas, during 1885 – six black servant girls and two upper-class socialites. A man called Nathan Elgin was originally a suspect. His right foot, which was missing a toe, matched some footprints left at the crime scene. Police officer John Bracken shot Elgin during a fracas with a girl in a bar, so of course, he wasn't charged with any crime. The ladies involved in the 'double event' on Christmas Eve left husbands who were charged with their murders but set free following a hung jury. No more murders occurred, therefore nothing more was done and the 'Midnight Assassin' – as he came to be known – faded into obscurity. We know the 'Midnight Assassin' to be James Maybrick.

"He returned to Liverpool, took up lodgings in Middlesex Street here in Whitechapel and, as you know, continued what he had started in Austin with our blessing. Nichols, Chapman, Stride, Eddowes, and Kelly, all fell under his knife. We have reason to believe Martha Tabram and Emma Smith may have also been Maybrick's, but we have been unable to substantiate it."

"And that brings us up to date, Mr Duggan, but it doesn't explain to me why you feel we have to expedite our plans for his removal."

Duggan nodded and continued. "We have had his wife under surveillance for some time and are assured she knows nothing about our involvement with her husband. In addition, Quinn's involvement with her has maintained that level of discretion. However…"

Archard waited a moment before pushing indignantly. "…well?"

"However, it has come to light that he may have been keeping a journal of his nocturnal proclivities." Duggan took a small step back as he finished the sentence, predicting the response.

"A journal?" Archard questioned flatly. "Interesting. And we know this how?"

Having been prepared for an explosive reaction, his employer's calm tone only added to Duggan's sense of unease. "Alice Yapp, the children's nanny, alerted us to its possible existence and claims to have seen it, but was unwilling to provide further details."

Archard's expression remained stoic. "She is one of your liaisons?"

Duggan nodded. "She had been in my confidence for some time before gaining employment with the Maybricks."

"So, the real question is whether this 'journal'– if it does exist – has any mention of us within its pages? I don't need to remind you what would happen if we were to be in any way connected to these crimes in Whitechapel. I have spent my entire life working towards what we are trying to do here. This society is broken, and if we don't intervene now, it will collapse under the weight of its own hubris. Maybrick is a means to an end and the first step towards a new order, one that will wipe away the old and bring fortitude and resolve in the new millennium. The unfortunates of Whitechapel who have fallen under his hand were necessary detritus to drive society towards our light. He was always expendable but became disposable the moment he butchered Kelly. If rumours of this journal are true, then we need to act quickly to rid ourselves of him. Do you believe Quinn's plan will succeed?"

Duggan was quick to acknowledge Archard's question. "Undoubtedly. I have been made privy to it, and I must admit it is quite clever. He seems unusually driven towards achieving some closure with Maybrick. Nevertheless, his plan, if successful, will both rid us of Maybrick and ensure no suspicion falls upon us should questions be asked."

"All that remains then," Archard conceded, "is for us to confirm this journal's existence, and if it implicates us in any way, dispose of it."

"I understand," Duggan acquiesced.

Archard turned his attention back to the folder on his desk and proceeded to flick through it again. Duggan waited a few moments before realising that his time in his employer's presence had ended. He turned and spun on his heels, before leaving the room. Nodding to the servant outside the door, he made his way down the stairs and outside.

Some of the trees lining the streets were mauve with signs of the oncoming winter. Horse-drawn carriages bumped past him on the cobbled streets as he made his way towards Quinn's lodgings, contemplating his plan. Upon Quinn's return visit to Florence Maybrick, he would request Quinn make a point of confirming this journal's existence and locate it if possible. They had to know whether Maybrick had implicated them.

He skirted around the prostitutes leaving The Ten Bells, ignoring their catcalls for his attention. He found the human cattle of Whitechapel fascinating and repellent at the same time. Though Maybrick seemed to have lost control, Duggan had to admit he was doing the country a favour by removing these wretched women from society. All that remained now was to remove him from the equation, and a cyclic sense of justice would have been achieved. They would, of course, honour his sacrifice, ensuring that history remembered what he had done and what The Brethren had accomplished.

James Maybrick could be the first of many.

"You create allegiance above your sworn allegiance to protect humanity. You shall not care for them, or acknowledge their pain. There lies the madness."
Murder by Decree

Quinn stood at the front door of Battlecrease House, awaiting a response to his knocking.

He turned to take in the view, admiring the Mersey at its most beautiful point from where the slope of the second highest of Liverpool's seven hills. The grounds encompassed acres, dotted with huge oak trees and many summerhouses, militantly patrolled by a pair of peacocks. He had to admit the view was majestic and uninterrupted, sweeping down to the Mersey and towards the mountains of Wales on the horizon. His reverie was broken by the sound of the door behind him. A housekeeper stood protectively in the opening, staring at Quinn quizzically.

"May I help?" she asked.

"Good morning," Quinn replied playfully. "I am here to speak with the lady of the house. Is she available?"

The housekeeper maintained her gaze, considering a response. "Mrs Maybrick is currently unavailable. May I ask the nature of your business?"

"I met with your employer a week or so ago and, being in the area, I thought I would pay her a return visit."

The housekeeper looked behind her momentarily as though listening out for something before turning back to face Quinn. "Come in," she instructed him apprehensively, ushering him into the foyer.

"Wait here, please," she then advised before heading off towards the rear of the house.

Quinn spun around slowly, marvelling at the grand décor and expansive ceilings. A huge stained-glass window dappled sunlight onto the pine staircase and the floor ahead of him, causing him to shift his gaze towards the massive, folding doors which he could see led to what appeared to be a ballroom.

Being a serial killer ala cotton merchant obviously has its advantages, Quinn thought to himself.

He didn't notice the black eye at first, due to Florence entering the hallway from the rear and remaining partially bathed in shadow.

"You should not be here, Mr Quinn. My husband doesn't take kindly to my being in the company of men without his presence," Florence stated quietly.

"My purpose for being here is solely to propose a secure future for you and your children," Quinn advised confidently. "Your husband knows myself and my associates very well, so his opinion is inconsequential."

"If only I could share your confidence," Florence whispered as she moved forward into the light. Quinn remained stoic in the presence of her appearance, already aware of Maybrick's penchant for violence. Yet, seeing the blackened areas around Florence's eyes and mouth caused him to momentarily feel protective towards her. He had never understood why a woman would remain with a man who would cause her harm. Granted, there must be an element of fear attached to any motivation to leave them, namely fear of repercussions. But to see such a beautiful woman violated in such a way only strengthened Quinn's resolve to ensure Maybrick suffered for his actions. It was just a shame that her sacrifice was integral to his plan, a conceit that caused him to feel a momentary pang of guilt.

Florence ushered Quinn into the next study, turning her face away slightly in embarrassment. Directing him to sit, she took the chair opposite and looked at him hesitantly.

"Please be brief, Mr Quinn," Florence pleaded. "Despite your assurance, I would rather James never knew you were here."

Quinn nodded his understanding. "Forgive my bluntness, but your husband is not who you think he is. He has secrets, dark secrets that threaten to destroy you, your family and potentially this country if left unchecked."

"This country!" Florence scoffed. "He's a cotton merchant who has many faults, but no secrets, except the lovers he thinks I do not know about."

Quinn smiled sadly. "How well do you know him, Florence?"

"I would thank you to refer to me as Mrs Maybrick."

Quinn ignored her and continued. "Where does he go when on his 'business' trips? What are his activities? Do you know where he has been spending his evenings while in London? Do you know he keeps a journal of his behaviour?"

Florence laughed nervously at Quinn's implication. "He tells me nothing of his business, and I know nothing of any journal. It is not my place to ask."

"But you should… you really should. You read the newspaper, yes? You know of the murders occurring in Whitechapel?"

Florence stared at Quinn for a few moments while contemplating a response. "What does any of that have to do with James?"

"Oh, my dear," he mocked. "It has everything to do with him."

"Are you saying that my husband is involved in those horrific occurrences?" Florence questioned incredulously.

Quinn smiled slightly. "I only ask you consider the evidence before you and then ask yourself again if your husband keeps no secrets." He rose from the chair and moved towards the front door. "I came to present you with a proposal, so here it is," Quinn said as he turned to face Florence, aware that what he was about to say would be deemed a betrayal of The Brethren's trust. But after seeing what Maybrick had done to her and aware he would likely do it again, he felt he had a moral obligation. It's what his wife would have wanted. "I can keep you safe, both you and your children from your husband and from what is soon to occur, but only if you accept it immediately. My offer expires once I leave and you should know that the consequences will be severe should you decline it."

Florence's face softened for a moment, as though considering his proposal but almost as immediately became stoic again. "Threatening a lady is most unbecoming of a gentleman, Mr Quinn. Please leave, or it will be I who alerts my husband."

Despite showing no visible apprehension at her threat, Quinn simply nodded and opened the door. He turned to her a final time, a sad smile on his face.

"You have my sympathies."

"For what?" Florence asked impatiently.

"For what is about to befall you."

Pulling the door closed gently behind him, Florence stared at where Quinn had been stood, his warning appearing to echo around the large hallway. Her once perfect life was crumbling around her, Quinn's allegations seeming more real in the cold shadow of her home. She refused to believe her husband was a killer, yet her heart told her she knew he was capable of great violence and fury.

Florence collapsed to the floor, her lips trembling and eyes welling as the fear and sadness bottled up inside her forced its way out. She pressed a hand to her mouth to stifle her heaving sobs. She knew she could never leave him. Whether Quinn was lying to scare her or speaking fact, she knew James would kill her before he let her go.

Squeezing her eyes shut, she took some deep breaths and thought. She would keep her children safe, no matter the lengths she had to go to. No matter what she had to do. Yet all the while, Quinn's words echoed around her head.

'Your husband is not who you think he is.'

———

Quinn leaned against the wall, listening intently for any sign his presence on the grounds had been detected.

He had returned to his lodgings after leaving Florence and waited until nightfall before returning to Battlecrease. Treading carefully through the plants and shrubs, he had made sure he stayed clear of the peacocks still making their rounds and had taken up a position at the rear of the house where he now waited.

Duggan had visited Quinn early that morning and tasked him with uncovering whether or not the journal existed – a journal that had a possible reference to his employers and their part in Maybrick's actions. His visit to Florence had failed to confirm its existence; however, Duggan had ultimately proven useful with this issue.

Duggan had informed him that his contact within the Maybrick household, though he had been reluctant to name her, had told him the journal was more than likely in the study, locked in a drawer. Where the study was located, outside of being on the first floor, was a detail Duggan had neglected to provide. That left Quinn with the challenge of searching the upstairs of Battlecrease without being discovered. Knowing from Florence's comments that her husband was home, the task had immediately become more challenging.

He took a final glance around him. The grounds were a tapestry of black and grey as afternoon gave way to evening, blurring the details of his immediate surroundings. Satisfied he remained unseen, he stepped up on to the window ledge and began his careful climb up the rear of the house. In the background the pulsating sound of Liverpool carried through the air, its harmony of noise, plaited voices and miasmas of sound applauding his ascent. Quinn felt confident that his time in the military, though not having taught him housebreaking nor mountaineering, had provided him with the instinct and precision to ensure success.

Reaching the first floor, he peered through the window. Light from the landing bled into the room – no one was present.

Hoping the window wasn't secured, he smiled inwardly when it easily slid open. Though it appeared too small to accommodate his entry, by hunching his shoulders he was able to twist through the opening. Dropping the short distance to the floor, he quietly closed the window behind him and waited in the silence. Once again, he heard nothing that would suggest he had been seen.

The room welcomed him with gloom. Quinn paused momentarily with his back to the window, his eyes adjusting to the shadow. When he was satisfied he wasn't going to bump into anything, he moved towards the door. His sweaty fingers slipped initially on the brass handle, forcing him to acknowledge how nervous he actually was.

Quinn closed his eyes and took a series of deep breaths and held them deep in his lungs before exhaling. Though his heart rate remained elevated, the extra intake of oxygen afforded him the ability to use his excellent motor skills once again. He turned the handle slowly until he heard the requisite click and opened it enough to allow him to see the full expanse of the landing and the rooms upon it. Raised, muffled voices drifted up the passage – a man and a woman.

He moved along the landing, glancing furtively around him. Quinn recognised Florence as one of the voices up ahead. The other – the man's – was Maybrick. Though it was difficult for him to make out, he managed to catch that Florence was refusing to believe something he was telling her, saying that he was only trying to scare her into leaving him. He heard her tell him he needed help before the voices became quieter, as though moving to another part of the room.

Quinn felt a momentary flash of fear. The realisation had come upon him that he was breaking into the house of a man who was a serial killer. He quickly reassessed his situation to accommodate the fact that underestimating Jack the Ripper would be a fatal mistake.

He listened intently. Making certain the voices remained distant, he tried the first door beside him. Glancing around, even in the darkness, he could see it was the children's nursery. The toys strewn on the floor seemed incongruous when considered alongside the man who was their father.

He pulled it shut and moved to the next door on the

opposite side of the corridor. Silently cursing to himself to find it was a bathroom, he closed the door and slid along the wall to the next possibility. Two rooms remained on this floor, one of which was the recipient of the still-raised voices echoing down towards him. He could only hope that they weren't arguing in the room he was looking for.

He uttered a silent prayer before trying the next door. The flicker of an oil lamp from an adjacent room cast an ominous luminosity over the surroundings. Bathed in orange silhouettes, Quinn could see a bed, a dresser and two doors opposite each other. He moved forward to find that the one to his right was a bathroom. He quickly walked to the remaining door and opened it slowly, trying to balance the anticipation of success with the disappointment of failure.

He found the anteroom minimalistic, with only a bureau, a chair and a chest of drawers. He stepped towards the bureau, confident that Maybrick and his wife remained in the other room from their distant voices. A sense of calm descended over him, bathing him with the assurance that he was in the right place. Trying the centre drawer, he was unsurprised to find it locked. He quickly looked through the cupboards on either side of the drawer to see them containing nothing of interest. He felt sure the item he was looking for was in the locked drawer as Duggan's contact had stated.

Quinn scanned the top of the bureau, looking for something he could use to spring the lock. Grabbing the fountain pen from its inkwell, he checked over the nib. It looked thinly pressed, meaning that it shouldn't be as stiff as the convex kind.

For the second time this evening, he prayed for good fortune as he worked the nib of the pen into the lock and began rotating it slowly, trying to feel for it catching the pin on the shear line. After what seemed like an eternity, he felt the trigger catch, causing it to disengage the lock on the drawer.

The snap and the click of the pin was not loud, but in the silence seemed thunderous. Realising he was holding his breath, Quinn let it out in a prolonged sigh. He could feel the sweat running down his back.

Placing the pen on the desk, he pulled open the drawer. Its only occupant was a dark blue, cross-grain leather, quarter bound guard book. Quinn stood and placed it on the desk, opening it carefully as though it were an object precious to him. Its discovery represented his dangerous mission here, and potentially the accolade of his peers should his information turn out to be accurate.

He opened the front cover, noting some oblong impressions on the flyleaf. He thought it looked more like a book used to hold photographs rather than a journal, though flicking to the next page he could see handwritten text and dates, confirming that it was indeed something that Maybrick was using as a record of events.

Quinn scanned the first page, noting lines crossed out, blots and smudges everywhere. It was only when he began to read the text further on that the mental state of the man they had taken into their employ became clear.

'I had read about my latest, my God the thoughts, the very best. I left nothing of the bitch, nothing. I placed it all over the room, time was on my hands, like the other whore I cut off the bitches nose, all of it this time. I left nothing of her face to remember her by.'

He flicked through more of the journal, seeing reference to the murders in America. The tone of the writing seemed to vary from deliberate to almost frenzied… the ravings of a madman. Having met the man, Quinn found it easy to believe that he was mentally ill.

The journal simply confirmed it.

Focusing on what he had been sent to discover, Quinn began to look in earnest for any reference to his employers. He had flicked forward a few pages before he saw them mentioned.

Duggan had been right. Maybrick was not only keeping a journal of his crimes but of his activities and those involved.

He scanned further for more references but found none. It appeared he had only mentioned them twice, in the first third of his writings. Quinn gave the journal one last look, before settling back in the chair to consider his next move.

His task had been to prove the journal's existence. Now that was confirmed, he needed to decide what to do about it. Quinn knew he couldn't take it. Once Maybrick discovered the journal missing he would surely suspect them, especially given their most recent meeting. Leaving it there wasn't a desirable option, but he had little choice, at least not at this moment.

The footsteps he heard moving towards his location forced him to act. Quickly rising from the chair, he dropped the book back into the drawer and quietly closed it, immediately having the fountain pen in hand to jam back into the lock. He flicked the pen from side to side, waiting for the sound of the pins clicking back into place. Footsteps arose outside the room, causing Quinn to twist the pen quicker. The lock clicked shut, and the bedroom door swung open simultaneously, boot heels ringing off the wooden floor and towards the bathroom he had seen moments earlier.

Quinn lunged across the room and took up a position behind the door before peering around it cautiously. A figure stood outlined in the glow from the landing light. He recognised the man as Maybrick even without seeing his face. He was standing still, making Quinn wonder if his presence had been detected and the madman was playing a game with him. Seconds seemed to stretch into minutes before the figure moved towards the bathroom and closed the door. Quinn knew he couldn't stay where he was. He had no idea where Maybrick would go next when he left the bathroom and, if he moved towards the study, Quinn would be trapped.

Knowing he had little time, he moved towards the still-open door and, checking the hallway was clear, walked quickly towards the room where he had first gained entry. No longer worried about making noise, Quinn moved into the room and closed the door behind him. Standing in the gloomy silence, he stepped towards the window but upon reaching it, stopped and leaned against the wall.

His legs felt weak, quivering as though he had been running for miles. He felt nauseated, almost on the brink of collapsing. He took a few moments before sliding open the window. The cold breeze and noise from outside roused him almost instantly, reaffirming his need to be out of the house and into the streets where he could feel safe.

He climbed onto the ledge and slid the window shut behind him. The ground seemed blurred and out of focus. He realised it was the adrenaline still pumping through his body in a flight or fight response. Taking a few deep breaths, he turned around and began the short climb towards the ground. Whether through a desire to be distant from the house, or sheer luck, he found every handhold and finger gap he needed to make it down in a matter of minutes.

Once on the ground, Quinn broke into a jog and hurried down the driveway and onto Riversdale Road. People glared at him as he barged past them, his need to have distance between him and Battlecrease House overriding his understanding that he shouldn't be drawing attention to himself. He needed to be back in London – back where he felt safest.

Gas lamps lit his way as he moved onto Aigburth Road and down towards the River Mersey. In the evening gloom, machinations began to coalesce in Quinn's mind, slowing, changing from random thoughts to a considered plan. He knew the consequences once The Brethren discovered his deceit regarding his relationship to Catherine Eddowes. He had needed their resources to dispose of Maybrick – something not originally part of their plan, but necessary now he had become a threat to them – which had made it easier for Quinn to do what he had to do. Where once he would have been acting alone, now he was amongst their ranks, being used as their tool for an act that served his purpose also. If he could obtain it, the journal would give him leverage to stop them from exacting punishment for his perfidy.

He felt guilt again with the realisation that Florence would be the one who suffered the most grievous consequences for their actions – his actions. But he had come too far to stop now. His desire for revenge had become an abscess on his soul, festering as though infected, with the only effective antibiotic that of justice.

Human vindictiveness, betrayal and treachery… acts that surpassed any rapprochement.

The streets around him bustled with people as he moved closer to the town centre, making it easy for him to believe that all was right with the world. But Quinn knew better. He was party to loosing a monster onto the earth. A beast who had, with their help, taken great pleasure in ripping women open and basking in The Brethren's protection.

A monster that would not forgive their betrayal lightly. He hoped the price was worth it.

"No man amongst you is fit to judge… the mighty art that I have wrought. Your rituals are empty oaths you neither understand nor live by. The Great Architect speaks to me. He is the balance where my deeds are weighed and judged… not you."
From Hell

24TH NOVEMBER, 1888
BATTLECREASE HOUSE, AIGBURTH.
LIVERPOOL

THE RAIN POUNDED RELENTLESSLY ON THE WINDOW AS Florence lay in the dark considering how her life could have ended up so complicated… so terrifying.

This time of night had become the most wretched time in the world for her when she found herself feeling more alone than she could have imagined possible.

The horrific things James had told her that night had played over and over in her mind a thousand times to the point that she was persistently nauseated. His claims that he was the man the press was calling Jack the Ripper had, at first, seemed ridiculous. She knew that he wanted to be rid of her so he could be with his mistress, whomever she was. Florence had initially believed his claims of being a murderer were just a dramatic pretence to get rid of her.

Yet, she knew of his darkness. His violent temper was something she had experienced first-hand on many occasions. So could she really convince herself he was a man incapable of murder and simply a loving father, albeit a poor husband? Even if it happened to be true, could she do what he had asked of her?

The empty space beside her in the bed only lent to her feelings of dread as to where he could be at this late hour.

Her thoughts turned to those poor unfortunates who had been butchered at the hands of Jack the Ripper. The very idea that she had possibly been sleeping with the man who had torn those women to pieces filled her with guilt and loathing. Had she known, there would have been little action she could have taken, but the fact that he was her husband made her feel complicit in any event.

Florie climbed from the bed, her intention to visit the bathroom, but instead, she found herself moving to the darkest corner of the room and sliding down the wall to the floor, shaking uncontrollably.

The reality of her situation hit her like an unrelenting tide. Her stomach rolled as she recalled Quinn's offer of help. He had known, hadn't he? Acidic burning rose in her chest, the bitter taste of gastric secretions filling the back of her mouth. She suppressed the urge to vomit, feeling the panic rise in her chest. Her mind reeled. Her life had suddenly taken on a drowning depth of stillness, as though the future was now frozen in a pent-up encapsulation of potential raw, explosive power. Waiting upon a decision to release it, for good or ill.

A thousand thoughts raced through her mind, actions, consequences, and priorities. They became a blur, making her head spin and forcing her to race to her predetermined location as the urge to vomit became overwhelming. As she retched up bile, something within her changed. Her accumulation of thoughts had suddenly become clear, as though they had chosen to stop on a particular suggestion like horses on a merry-go-round.

It would be hard, she had no doubt. He was the father

of her children. If she left him, his standing would remain in the upper echelons of Liverpool society. She would be the harlot… the adulteress who abandoned her husband and children. His pursuit of her would yield little reward. Yet she would lose her children. The very idea of it made Florie feel both guilt and extreme sadness. But if she took them with her, then he would never stop in his pursuit. And when he found her, if he were indeed the man the press was calling Jack, what would he do?

No, she knew the only way to be truly free was if she decided to follow this course of action. Florie had seen the torment in his eyes when he had asked her to help him end it all, as though a great battle were raging within him for his very soul. Whether because of his addiction or his claims of murder, Florie was uncertain, as uncertain as she was about what she had been asked to do. A modicum of solace could be found in that it had been his request. And now that the chance of escaping him, by whatever means, had settled into her head, she found herself daring to feel a glimmer of hope.

Hope, she prayed, that her future wasn't predestined.

Quinn stared at the flaking ceiling in his small room. At five shillings and sixpence, you couldn't really expect much more than the bed, washbasin, peeling décor and rising damp. It all contributed to his already oppressive mood.

The silence was deep, which Quinn found unusual for Whitechapel but comforting nevertheless. He usually could hear raucous drunks leaving their preferred drinking houses, carriages clattering throughout the streets and, occasionally, the sounds of men with their temporarily purchased escorts groaning with a salacious passion up against his outside wall. But not tonight. Tonight, the wind was abed, and the whole of London seemed still as though pensively waiting for something to happen.

Discovering the journal had been unexpected, as he hadn't been entirely convinced of its existence. But due to Maybrick's messianic belief in his mission and narcissistic personality, his desire to document his actions meant that Quinn now had the first thing he needed to secure his own safety from The Brethren's wrath in case they discovered his deceit.

The second thing he needed to do was expedite his plan to dispose of the Ripper.

Quinn knew the man was addicted to arsenic. Maybrick's general practitioner, Richard Humphrey, was in The Brethren's employ. He had advised them that while attending to one of the children for whooping cough, Florence had informed him that her husband was taking a 'white powder' which initially the doctor assumed to be strychnine but later discovered to be arsenic. Given his highly addictive personality, Quinn knew that he would almost certainly still be taking it.

Maybrick was now an untenable risk, one the organisation could not afford to indulge any longer. An overdose would be reasonably straightforward, his death releasing any hold he thought he had over them owing to their complicity in his actions. By default, Quinn would also be provided with the justice he craved so desperately. He had grown to despise his employers because of their active involvement and ignorance at the monster's butchery.

His thoughts momentarily shifted towards his wife, the sadness almost immediately overwhelming before being replaced by something else. Upon discovery that his employers knew the Ripper's identity, Quinn had been incensed. They dared to justify their ignorance of Maybrick's actions by claiming it was for the benefit of society. That he was helping forward their cause of destabilising the monarchy and societal strata for them to manoeuvre into critical positions for the greater good.

Quinn, through obfuscation and inveiglement, had discovered many of their secrets and plans for the future, plans which lay the groundwork for the next hundred years. Their ultimate goal was to have many facets to their organisation under the pretence of being humanitarians and advocates of justice. Though their use of Maybrick had initially seemed capriciously incongruous to this agenda, Quinn had slowly realised that they saw him as a tool whose atrocious acts could be used as a legacy for promotional purposes. Allow him to commit his crimes, satiate his desires, disappear into the mists of time and then use his legacy to promote a new world order, one with them as leaders in the field of justice and societal reconstruction.

Jack the Ripper had helped put their ideology into action.

It was odious and distasteful in the extreme, but they were providing Quinn with the means to get close enough to Maybrick in order to achieve their mutual goal.

His plan would need to be implemented carefully, and with patience so as not to draw suspicion. Even then, Quinn knew he would need something more to assuage The Brethren from looking too closely. Something in the shape of a suspect.

Florence was already close to breaking point. He saw it in her face that morning at the house – fear, anger, desperation. Quinn knew she would welcome a release from his overbearing, obsessive hold over her.

Quinn could arrange to surreptitiously increase his

arsenic intake slowly over time. The Brethren had people in their employee he could exploit. Maybrick's body would soon fail him, questions would be asked, and fingers would be pointed at the abused wife, obviously pushed towards murder. Though Quinn felt guilt at the thought of the children without a mother, he knew it was the only way. He had offered to help her, but she had rebuffed him.

What happened next was on her.

'Jack the Ripper. A rubric name that glistens in the black pantheon of criminal legend. He must be the best-known, unknown murderer in the world. In his continuing anonymity lies his enduring fame. More ink has been spilt on him than blood flowed in all his murders: millions and millions of words, which, if placed end to end, would stretch from here to… nowhere.'
Stephen Knight – The Final Solution

11TH MAY, 1889 BATTLECREASE HOUSE, AIGBURTH. LIVERPOOL

Dr William Carter glanced back briefly to see Maybrick's closest friend cradling his lifeless body.

He closed the door quietly behind him, muffling the sound of the man's sobbing.

He nodded at Richard Humphreys, the second attending physician currently consoling one of the servants before moving towards the adjacent room where Florence had been carried after collapsing earlier that morning. She was oblivious as to what had just occurred, and William Carter didn't think he wanted to be the one to tell her when she awoke that her husband was dead. In fact, he wasn't sure whether he wanted to speak to her at all.

Eight days earlier, he and Humphreys had attended Maybrick at his brother Edwin's request. They had found him in great distress, complaining of stomach cramps and what he termed a 'hair' in his throat. They had both agreed he was suffering from dyspepsia, prescribing something to relieve his throat discomfort and accompanying treatments to help ease the foul taste he was complaining of in his throat. With instructions to Florie that his diet should be restricted to chicken broth and milk, they had left hopeful that whatever was ailing him would settle enough to allow him to get some rest. This had all been although they were aware Florie had previously obstructed attendance of a doctor to her husband because he would not "do what they said anyway".

It was a few days later, and following the hiring of Nurse Gore from the Queen's Nursing Institute in Liverpool, that the doctors were advised Maybrick's wife was suspected of foul play concerning her husband's malady. The suspicions were given to them by Alice Yapp who had been made privy to the contents of a letter Florie had asked her to post. Carter hadn't asked how she happened to know what the letter said, though Yapp had said she had accidentally dropped it in a puddle and, asking the Post Office to provide her with a clean envelope, had caught sight of some of it while swapping them over.

She had advised them that the letter was obviously to Florie's lover and that it had made reference to something Maybrick had told her which she believed preposterous and only intended to frighten her.

And now there was the suspicion that Florie had been tampering with her husband's medicine bottles amidst claims that she had been seen soaking flypapers known to contain arsenic. Carter refused to believe that Florie was responsible for poisoning her husband. He had already tested urine and faecal samples, along with a bottle of Neaves Foods provided by Maybrick's other brother, Michael, under the pretence that she had tampered with them. All turned out to be negative. He also found Michael's accusations odd given that, as arsenic was so easy to purchase, the soaking of flypapers to extract the drug would be quite laborious. Despite that, now that he was dead it seemed the whole household, from Maybrick's two brothers Edwin and Michael to the kitchen staff, believed Florie was responsible.

No, when she awoke, he did not want to speak to her. After all, what could he say that would make her feel any better with what was likely to occur?

Quinn stood in the street, looking up at Battlecrease House. The activity he had observed in and out of the house told him that death was either circling Maybrick or had already occurred. Granted it would be a good death compared to that of his wife's, but then again a good end was as ambiguous as it was eclectic, a concept beset with paradox and tension. Death may have embraced him, but it will have been a slow, painful experience.

He stared at the house, admiring it for a moment as though appraising a priceless antique. In a society that his employers were ensuring span away from ochlocracy and towards a form of capitalism governed by themselves, Quinn realised he was approaching the nadir of his journey. Maybrick's death would free him from the guilt he had carried for what seemed like forever – the sin of a man unable to protect his family. Never once had he given up on the hope that fate would allow him a chance at redeeming what he thought he had lost – control.

Maybrick had taken the ability to govern his own life from him, leaving him feeling only inadequacy and powerlessness. He had deceived and manipulated The Brethren and Florence to regain a modicum of control over his life, and though he felt guilt at what was likely to befall Florie, he believed he was on the side of the righteous. The justice that the police and Abberline had been unable to provide him would be served.

He only needed Carter to keep his end of the bargain and supply him with the journal. Getting hold of it shouldn't be difficult with the good doctor also in the employee of The Brethren. Whether Carter knew of its contents mattered little to Quinn. The only constant had to be Florence. She had to remain the only suspect. Guilty beyond a reasonable doubt – beaten, humiliated and pushed to breaking point by a violent man who had left her no choice but to act to preserve herself and her children.

Giving the journal to Quinn would ensure the identity of

Jack the Ripper remained lost amidst rumours, conjecture and supposition. That would suit The Brethren and him perfectly.

Tampering with Maybrick's medicine had been relatively straightforward. It was pure coincidence that Florie had been noted as purchasing and soaking fly papers to coincide with her husband's determination to end his own life. Whether her purpose for buying them was for makeup, clothes dye or another purpose mattered little. The very fact they had been discovered, alongside the suspected tampering of the medicine bottles and the well-known suffering she had endured, would make her the primary focus of any investigation. It might even aid him once The Brethren discovered his deception, with the journal acting as extra leverage.

Quinn wondered if they would applaud his initiative should his motives remain hidden. He had freed the world from Jack the Ripper, an acknowledgement worthy of prestige in the hallowed halls of The Brethren. Whatever the outcome, any discovery that he held the journal would send a clear message.

Left alone, he would keep secret the fact that they gave birth to a monster.

"The police were no nearer to capturing the monster that lurked in the crevices, and London seemed stiller in the dark, the streets devoid of hope."
Carol Oates – Something Wicked

18TH JULY, 1908 ST. OLAVE'S WORKHOUSE, BERMONDSEY

THE ATMOSPHERE WAS POISONED WITH THE SOUND OF torment and the smell of excrement.

The latter was a consequence of the water closet overflowing in the infirm department, the former due to the wretched souls held there in perpetuity, forever dammed. Dante's words had never been apter to suggest that all those who entered here were to abandon even hope. Sebastian Archard felt filthy merely being in the building, yet his visit need not be extended. He only needed a few moments with the patient to be assured.

The stout orderly, who had failed to introduce himself, silently gestured Archard in the direction of a long, narrow corridor off the main thoroughfare of the hospital. The workhouse itself formed a rough square, the building Archard was currently in having been erected in 1791 due to an increase in demand. Looking as though it had thrust itself up from the very stony soil, it sat on to become a natural formation, St. Olave's consisted of a porters lodge, dining hall, kitchens and the guardian's boardroom. The male inmates were accommodated alongside the west of the building. It was there that Archard would find the reason for his visit.

"May I ask why it's him ya wish ta see, Sir?" the orderly asked.

"It is a sensitive matter so I would appreciate it if myself and the patient could have some privacy," Archard replied curtly.

The orderly sucked air across his bottom lip disapprovingly. "I'm not allowed to do that, Sir. He's been known to be violent, I'd be fer the sack if anything 'appened to you."

Archard stopped walking and spun to face the steward. "You will do as I ask and remain outside until I tell you otherwise. Is that understood?"

Taken aback by the peremptory edict, the orderly hesitated before replying. "As ya wish, Sir."

The atmosphere became more oppressive as they moved further into the sepulchral workhouse, as though the entreaties of the damned had become tangible and were polluting the air around them. Archard had been under the impression that the standards had improved since The Lancet investigation into workhouse conditions, but as far as he could see the place was still a fever-nest for epidemics. He cared little if he was honest, the pathetic examples of humanity residing here only serving to reinforce his belief that society was crumbling and needed to be rebuilt.

If it was on the souls of those around him, so be it.

The orderly stopped outside a single room and removed the keys from his belt. "As I warned, he can be violent at times, especially since his 'ead was cut open. Strange bloke, stranger than most o' the ones we get in 'ere. Been ramblin' on since he came 'ere that he knew the identity of Jack the Ripper and other odd things. Well, that was until they spiked his 'ead. Makes no sense most o' the time now. Anyways, I'll wait here till ya need me."

Archard nodded acknowledgement and stepped back, allowing the door to be unlocked. As he stepped inside, the orderly quickly closed it behind him as though afraid its occupant would be able to slip out.

The room was damp and smelled of a multitude of human odours, some of which Archard refused to even contemplate. Its only source of light was a small, barred window flush to the wall. It held a long, orange box that Archard could only assume was a bed, with a wooden log for a pillow. A blanket and rug hung over the bottom. The absence of even straw as padding made it look more like a torture device than something to sleep on.

A man was curled up in a foetal position in the corner against the wall muttering incoherencies, his chin glistening with saliva. His body occasionally twitched, straining against the filthy straitjacket binding his arms across his chest. Archard had expected the stereotypical rocking back and forth but, aside from the trembling, he was perfectly still. His hair was matted and greasy, the soles of his feet visibly lacerated and discoloured with congealed blood and dirt from the floor.

Archard stepped closer while at the same time maintaining a comfortable distance.

"Thomas, I would like to speak to you. Do you know who I am?"

The mumbling stopped immediately at the sound of the visitor's voice, Quinn's head turning slightly as though listening out for something specific.

"Can you understand me?" Archard continued. "It's quite important we talk."

"They all say that, don't they? It's always important, always important. Invalided from India with disease of the heart. Don't tell me what to do, she said. Catherine's coming with me, you can't see George or Thomas she said."

Archard ignored Quinn's nonsensical ramblings. "Thomas, I need you to pay attention. Do you remember me?"

Turning slowly to face him, Quinn stared blankly at Archard. The lobotomy puncture wound was visible on his forehead, his face waxy and swollen. His eyes, though glazed, appeared to register recollection of his visitor's identity.

"Dear Boss... the man who put me here. Jack's leash."

Ignoring the reference to one of the Ripper letters and sensing an opportunity, Archard knelt to crouch before Quinn. "There was a journal, Thomas. Do you remember the journal?"

Quinn elicited a deep laugh, all the while continuing to stare at his guest. Holds all your secrets, it does. Yours and his... yours and Jack's."

He turned his back to the wall and began to slide along it towards his makeshift bed. "I left nothing of her face to remember her by. I remember, never forget. A man telling tales of a monster... he loved her you know."

Frustrated, Archard leant over and grabbed Quinn by the face. "Tell me, man, where is it?"

"I never got it," he replied, becoming suddenly lucid. "Carter was supposed to get it for me... that was our deal. I got the journal, you left me alone. I did it for her... you didn't care. She was a shilling whore and meant nothing. But to me, she meant something. I waited for him that night and the ones after that, but I never got it."

Archard released his grip on Quinn's face and moved over to sit on the bed.

"You don't know where it is, do you?" Quinn asked

with a smirk. "After everything – her imprisonment, putting me in here – you still don't know. Poor Sebastian, poor Florie, poor Thomas…"

Archard stood and banged on the door, aware he would get nothing more from Quinn. He heard keys in the lock and pushed himself out as it had barely begun to open.

"Everythin' okay, Sir?" the orderly asked, but Archard had already pushed past him. His desperation to be away from the workhouse and its pathetic inhabitants were almost as urgent as his need to wash its stink off. He felt as though it had permeated his skin. His frustration and disappointment at coming away empty-handed only served to enhance the disparaging nature of the workhouse, though he knew he had a great deal to be pleased with.

The Brethren's manipulation of Maybrick had proven ultimately successful. With the ongoing controversy between the liberals and social reformers, alongside the Irish Home rule partisans, his crimes couldn't have come at a more opportune moment. The Times and The Daily Telegraph, not to mention

The Star had all stressed the danger the crimes posed to law and order, emphasising a need to alleviate the poverty causing crime. The whole situation had only confirmed Archard's belief that society was a crime and disease-ridden, uncivilised jungle full of semi-barbarians.

It was Maybrick's actions that had allowed Archard's vision to become a serious consideration in Parliament. His offer to ensure that the controversy surrounding Queen Victoria's grandson could be hidden had further assured him a seat. He now had all he needed to ensure The Brethren became a vital element of a new world reform – one where he could be king.

Quinn's claim to know the identity of Jack the Ripper

would be denounced as symptoms of his condition. Archard had ensured that any connection between him and The Brethren had been lost, leaving only the fact that the man currently residing in St. Olaves workhouse had been discharged from the 1st Battalion of the 18th Irish Regiment and had had three children. Though the removal of Maybrick and framing of his wife had been successful, Quinn's inability to secure the journal had sealed his fate and jeopardised The Brethren. For that incompetence, they had sent him here, where his claims of Jack the Ripper's identity would remain ignominious, as would claims of any governmental involvement.

Yet his visit here had forced Sebastian Archard to acknowledge a foundry emotion – an emotion he had learnt to ignore, but which this brief foray into human manipulation had reminded him to feel. Fear.

The very creation of The Brethren had been motivated by that most innate of emotions, yet at the same time, something he had steadfast refused to acknowledge. His fear of society's collapse and vision for the future had forced him to bury that fear deep, knowing that any acquiescence to it would devour him whole before his vision could become a realisation.

Inserting James Maybrick into their lives had made fear an authentic and tangible presence in his life, seeking to undo everything he had built. Archard had to admit his own hubris had blinded him to the risks and solipsistic traits of human beings. The journal held details of their involvement in his crimes. Should it become public knowledge, everything he was trying to accomplish would be undone. His thoughts turned to the wife and the part she had played in all of this. Since her release from prison four years earlier, Archard had ensured Florence was closely watched. The public had never truly believed

Florence had murdered her husband, convinced it must have been out of fear for her safety and that of her children.

Queen Victoria herself had saved her from the hangman's noose based purely on public opinion, instead of commuting her sentence to life in prison. Such clemency seemed later justified, with the judge who presided over Florence's case ending up in an insane asylum and the whole affair being subsequently used by the Court of Criminal Appeals as an example of how flawed the British justice system was.

It mattered little. Maybrick's wife served her purpose. Quinn and a small number of Archard 's close associates had ensured there was enough evidence to cast suspicion on Florence. Her arrest and conviction had allowed everything else to become lost in the media frenzy that followed. The last he had heard was that she was a virtual recluse, living in a squalid three- bedroom cabin in Connecticut, earning a living on the lecture circuit talking about injustice and working as a housekeeper. He didn't even think anyone had actually discovered her true identity.

Nevertheless, he remained suspicious of her, especially now. His gut feeling was that she had the journal or at least knew where it was. He had never bought the whole charming, Southern Belle persona and remained convinced they had perhaps underestimated her.

Despite his anxiety at the journal's absence, he had to commend Quinn for his ingenuity and even understood his motivation. No one had ever suspected the link. He was known to the world as Thomas Quinn, the same surname he used to draw his military pension. And this deception had ultimately become his undoing.

All because of a whore who had been his wife.

No one had known Quinn by his real name – Thomas Conway.

So no one had known his wife had been Catherine Eddowes, the fourth victim of Jack the Ripper.

Ultimately his actions had proven fruitless. Nothing could stand in the way of what was now in motion. If and when the journal was discovered, Archard would be in a position to deal with the problem. His organisation would build on its own inertia and ensure The Brethren became a power to be feared. And as for Maybrick, they had plans for him. His death would not prevent them.

As he made his way from the workhouse and into the sunlight, Sebastian Archard smiled at the realisation that it would be he, not a murderer, whom history would say gave birth to the twentieth century.

"I give my name that all know of me, so history do tell what love can do to a gentle man born. Yours truly, Jack the Ripper."
James Maybrick – The Diary of Jack the Ripper

THE TALE HE TOLD ME WAS A PURE FABRICATION AND ONLY intended to frighten the truth out of me.

The words echoed in her mind as though spoken yesterday.

The squalid three-roomed cabin was stark, with only the most basic of furnishings. The ghosts of her memories were her only company, alongside the many cats padding around the room or sleeping on various ledges and in cubbyholes.

Long before James had died, she had known her marriage was over in all but name, leaving her little motivation to kill him as they stated. Financially, the provision he had left for her and the children in his will was paltry. She would have been financially better off separated from him.

Yet they believed she had killed him, poisoned him with his own medicine. Everyone had ignored the fact he was addicted to arsenic and that the damage had already been done by his own hand over many years, the only evidence against her a tampered bottle and fly papers soaking in the kitchen.

Moving to America upon her release had offered some comfort. Her mother had stood by her while the world declared her a murderer, a killer who took her husband's life because he was about to divorce her. Maybe they thought it was because she would lose her children if they divorced. She no longer remembered.

He had asked her to kill him the night he had told her he was the Whitechapel murderer and, though she had wanted to do it out of both his desperation for release and her desire to be free of him, she could never have actually gone through with it. The cumulative effect of his years of arsenic abuse had caused his own abortion, yet she had been found guilty of his murder anyway.

The irony of the whole, sad situation was not lost on Florie.

She sat thoughtfully, the pen poised in her hand before she began writing again in the notebook on her lap.

'A time will come when the world will acknowledge that the verdict which was passed on me is absolutely untenable. But what then? Who shall give back the years I have spent within prison walls; the friends by who I am forgotten; the children to whom I am dead; the sunshine; the winds of heaven; my woman's life, and all I have lost by this terrible injustice?'

Florie had often considered whether refusing Quinn's offer had been a mistake. Given the circumstances of her husband's addiction, would they have felt her culpable anyway? Her suffering at his hands was no secret to many in Liverpool, leaving her at the mercy of people always believing she had good reason to retaliate. It appeared her years of torment had become the probable cause instead of her redemption. She had never seen or heard from Quinn again. Florie often wondered what had become of him.

Her trial had generated Florie a small number of supporters, particularly her lawyer Andrew Dawson and Joseph Levy. Levy's book, The Necessity for Criminal Appeal, focused solely on her case stating that her trial was 'one of the most extraordinary miscarriages of justice of modern times' and that though her moral guilt of James's murder was probable, her verdict of guilt was as questionable as the affirmation that she was provided with a fair trial.

As welcome as this support was, Florie had still lost fourteen years of her life as number LP29 in Woking and Aylesbury prison and had not seen or heard from her children since her incarceration in January. The reprieve from execution had only secured her solitary confinement, hard labour and frequent illness in a tiny, unlit cell. Fourteen years lost to an unjust justice system and because she fell in love with the wrong man.

All she had left was that most powerful of weapons – knowledge.

She knew of James's journal, his crimes and the part others had played in them. She had ensured it was hidden, sequestered in the last place anyone would think to look. The place she had once called home.

It was this secret that kept her warm at night and something she knew kept her safe. From whom and what she was uncertain. She suspected that the group of men James had referred to within the pages of the journal were people to be feared. Florie was unsure as to whether they related to the Masonic brotherhood he had been involved with or something else, but whoever it was he had alluded to within the journal's pages they had been party to his crimes. If they knew of him, they knew of her. The fact others shared knowledge of her husband's murderous indiscretions only served to exacerbate the journal's already horrific content. For that reason, she had separated the first third of the journal that referenced them and hidden it separately. If the journal were to one day be discovered, let history know of her husband's crimes. She had a feeling that those torn out pages and her suspicions were all that was keeping her alive.

James's knowledge of Alfred had obviously fuelled his crimes, something for which Florence felt guilt. Her indiscretion had caused the deaths of women, both here and abroad. She would never forgive herself for that. Ultimately, her quest for happiness had ended in despair, with Alfred severing contact with her after the conviction.

Everything prologue had become bitterness worse than death. But one day all would become clear. Florie knew justice had been denied her, and those poor women. Her husband had died a comfortable death unlike that which he had inflicted upon them. Vucetich and Galton's breakthrough in the use of fingerprints as a means of identification had been three years too late to provide justice for Nicols, Chapman, Stride, Eddowes and Kelly. The unfairness of it all stabbed at Florie's soul.

Her only comfort now was that history would make it right. Like a river blocked by a dam, eventually, water finds its way through.

Just like the truth.

Maybrick's family crest stated it eloquently.

'Tempus Omnia Revelat.'

Time Reveals All.

"Since then the idea has taken full possession of me, and everything fits in and dovetails so well that I cannot help feeling that this is the man we struggled so hard to capture fifteen years ago…"

Inspector Frederick Abberline

18TH SEPTEMBER, 1908 LOCATION UNKNOWN

THE CAVERN WAS VAST AND COLD.

Various pieces of equipment designed for digging were strewn about the floor, the furthest about sixty yards away indicating the cavern's size. The technician's footsteps echoed off the metallic roof some sixty stories above as he made some minor adjustments to the chamber in front of him. A slight fog had enveloped him and the platform he stood on, settling about his feet as he worked. The silence was broken only by the occasional hiss of venting gases and chemicals and his breathing.

The technology he was working with was unlike anything he had ever seen. Pulled from the Crescent Shipyard in Elizabeth, New Jersey, the year prior, George Sigler had been told by his mysterious benefactor that his work with Lewis Nixon was pivotal in what his company was trying to achieve.

'The future of constitutionality' had been his exact words. From submarines and sonar to working in secret in a dark, underground cavern somewhere even he didn't know the location of. Every day he was brought under light sedation; every day he left the same. His only instructions were to learn the technology and how to make more. More for what he didn't know, but he suspected it was for more of what was currently his only source of company.

The man looked as though he were asleep. Miasma swirled about his naked body, the extreme cold having caused crystallisation on his extremities but without any apparent damage to the tissue. George hadn't attempted to understand how it worked during his time here. He found the fact he was working on equipment housing a human body in some sort of suspended animation was grotesque and frightening in equal measure.

But he had been paid enough to see him and his family comfortable for the remainder of their lives, so any disquiet he felt at potentially being an accessory to something illegal he was happy to ignore. Study, learn, repeat had been his instructions. And that was precisely what he had been doing.

He had already started work on the second chamber, having felt comfortable he knew enough to commence the basic design. All the materials and equipment he needed were always ready the day following his request. He never saw anyone come and drop them off, nor did he see anyone leave.

Stepping down from the platform, George moved over to the workbench and put down his monitoring devices. He picked up the metal nameplate and breathed on it before buffing it with the sleeve of his jacket. His instructions for the typeset had been specific and short. Once again, he had contained his curiosity for fear of consequence.

Picking up some screws and a screwdriver, George walked back to the platform and climbed up the stairs. He moved around to the side of the chamber and selected what he thought was a good location for the plaque before securing it into position.

He had studied his companion every day but was none the wiser as to his identity. George certainly didn't recognise him. A few days ago, he had decided that when his work was complete, he might ask his employer for the man's name. He had no interest in what he had done, or why he was there. He only wanted a name so he could call him something other than 'fella'.

So maybe the plaque he had been left to fit was fortuitous. Now he had a name to call his only source of company. A name and what appeared to be a designation. George shrugged to himself as he stood back. Satisfied with the placement, he made his way off the platform and back to his workbench. There was plenty to do before they came for him.

"Subject One 1888,' he said out loud. "Aye, I think I'll just stick with Jack."

"I know and my superiors know certain facts. The Ripper wasn't a butcher, Yid or foreign skipper... you'd have to look for him not at the bottom of London society but a long way up."

Inspector Frederick Abberline

2ND OCTOBER, 2011 DUBLIN, IRELAND

"Your two o'clock has arrived, Sir."

"Show him in, Emily," Gideon Archard said in an insouciant tone. He had already turned back to the thick file on the desk before she had even begun moving out of his office.

Methodically scanning each page, he made one or two mental notes before closing the folder and leaning back in his chair, clasping his hands together by his mouth. Gideon was firm of the belief that understanding was the best preparation for what lay ahead. It had virtually been the family motto since his great-grandfather had created The Brethren back in 1888. Despotic he may have been, but a visionary he indeed was.

Even back then, Sebastian Archard had seen what the world needed to become to survive and the part they had to play in its apotheosis. The Brethren now consisted of some of the most powerful men and women on the planet, including leaders in world government and the private sector. Their business spanned across every continent.

They had more money than the World Bank could make in a year and their allegiances could affect sea change down to the minutiae of human existence – money, water, weapons, housing, commodities, the food that was eaten and the information that was dealt with to tell people what to think and who they really were.

All of this, and yet if what lay ahead was successful, it would be one of the organisation's greatest achievements.

The ringing phone broke his reverie at the same time a well-built man entered his office. He picked up the receiver and gestured his visitor toward the chair on the other side of the desk.

"It's me," the man on the other end of the line said. "I've just had a reporter asking to see the booking log for the night of Stark's execution. I didn't give him anything, and he seemed satisfied, but I don't know. You told me that no one would ask questions. This is my career on the line here. If I'd have known people were going to start poking around, I would have…"

Archard smiled at his precognition of the caller's next words and his apparent reluctance to say them. Instead, the sentence finished with, "What should I do?"

"Was it O'Connell?" Archard asked, lifting his gaze towards the man opposite him.

"How did you know?" came the puzzled response.

"Do nothing," Archard said, hanging up the phone before the man could respond.

His guest shifted forward in his seat, as though expecting instructions. "I gather we have a problem." It was a statement rather than a question. Milton knew he wasn't requested unless there was a situation that required his particular skill set to address.

"A particular individual is becoming tiresome,"

Archard replied. "I'd like you to see to it he has some car trouble."

"Does this person have a name," Milton asked.

"O'Connell," Archard stated. "Joe O'Connell.

In 1992, a document presented as James Maybrick's diary surfaced. In the diary, or journal, Maybrick took credit for slaying the five victims most commonly credited to Jack the Ripper as well as other murders which have to date not been historically identified.

The first third of the journal appeared to have been torn out, leading to much speculation as to its contents and what, if it is to be believed that Maybrick was truly Jack the Ripper, it may have suggested about his state of mind prior to those fateful nights in 1888.

Now, for the first time, you will see the secrets James Maybrick held and the actions that sent him on the path to become history's most notorious serial killer.

THE JOURNAL OF JAMES MAYBRICK

Molly was her name. Her head caved in like a
watermelon. My first and I found her exquisite.
The other servants were no challenge. That fool
lying beside the last of them was a gift. Women are
my mission but why not a man. It felt different.
Solid. His head didnt collapse like the others. It has
been to long so I begin again. I decided to write it
down to remember and so others could know
should this ever be found. I keep thinking of Bunny.
I truly believe I have been given a mission. To rid
the world of all whores. I am not done.

I feel I am preparing for what is to come. These
servant girls proved good for practice. They are
everywhere here so make easy pickings. No one
misses them. And no one suspects. The cotton
merchant hiding in plain sight – ha ha. I do believe
I am beginning to understand what it was I was
placed here to do. All whores will know soon
enough. My business can continue at home. But

not yet. I feel cold inside and miss my son. My
memories of him fade sometimes and it makes me
sad. I will see him soon.

I am ill tonight. I cannot stop shaking and the pain
keeps me awake. My medicine does little to quell
the cramps. I dream that I am being punished for
what I have done and what I intend to do. I know
not if keeping this journal is wise should it ever be
discovered it will destroy Bunny and Bobo. I know
only love drove me to this. Dear God make me well
enough to see my family.

The police here are bungling. They have no idea it
is i killing the whores. Uneducated servants. I feel
unfulfilled because they are so easy and
everywhere. The Midnight Assassin they call me –
ha ha. What a ridiculous name. I will have
something better to be remembered by. A name
known by all for all time. The whores will know
and be afraid. I look forward to tomorrow. I have
watched them. Black servants they are not.

On Christmas Eve Moses found the whore
    The other her brains decorated the floor

So they chose to celebrate the first ship from my
city coming here with flags and lights. 'God Save
The Queen' indeed. The bitch will soon know of
my work in her home. I almost laughed reading
that Moses had found her. Perhaps a message from
God. The other was softer. She groaned as though
being pleasured. It made me think of the whore. A
double event for that fool Grooms Leigh. Those

fools mention it to me and I show nothing ha ha.
They have no idea oh if they only knew. I have
been clever so very clever.

I made the double event here my last. The state of
Texas will remember what I did. Being ignorant to
the reason lessens the impact not. They say I raped
them the fools. I would not tarnish myself. The
knife and axe I rammed into them was pleasure
enough. I feel the need to do it again. But not here.
I need to be home. I have forced thoughts of
Bunny from my mind for too long. This gentle man
who needs to keep gentle thoughts. My medicine
will help calm the battle within me.

Am I not a clever fellow. They look to the footprints
but to me they will not lead.

Footprints left footprints right Footprints five
footprints four

I laugh knowing they cannot find me. The whores
let me see I am good at this a master no less. Sir
Jim is becoming a very clever fellow indeed.

The bitch Cranstoun would have me stop my
medicine. She told me it is to blame for my pains. I
cannot do without it. My hands grow so cold I
wonder if I would be able to hold the knife. I need
to be home now no more can I do here. The fools
see the cotton merchant and look past the man they
seek. My doubts vanish as to my purpose. This
place is becoming sour fruit.

I grow worried about my compulsion to write down my deeds. I fear it will be my undoing. It thrills me to write about how the whores split open but at night I wonder if I am doing wrong. I feel lost. Being so far from home makes it worse. I miss Bobo. Even my Bunny. May she forgive me on the day my deeds are discovered. When I return I need to rest. I am pained constantly. My medicine has no effect at times. At night I see their faces begging to be spared. May god forgive the man I have become.

It is decided. I will return to Grassendale. I will be able to decide where to start again. My deeds here have only served to prove I am a clever fellow. Indeed I am. They have no idea no idea and once home I will be far away. Perhaps Liverpool perhaps London. The whores there are many. I can use what I have learnt to become something more. And who shall they know me by. A name that will be remembered by all.

Sir Jim returns home to see the whores Sir Jim will open them wide Their blood will paint the cobbled floors ha ha ha

It has been too long. I have stayed my hand since returning home. The whores have remained safe but my desire for them to die only grows within me. I know now she has a whoremaster. Slowly the bitch poisons me poisons my soul. I maintain all sense of dignity for the masses but I am losing the battle I fight within. Bobo keeps me sane but soon I must be cutting again. Only feeling the whores rip wide will satisfy me.

The whore has hers and I have mine. She is a calming influence on me. I have no desire to hurt her. The bitch only drives me closer to her. How I would love to rip her wide in front of her whoremaster. The more time passes the more nervous I become about starting my campaign again. I must find the courage to continue. The whore must be made to suffer.

I have not seen Michael for some time. I must pay him a visit next time I am close by. Edwin too. How they would be surprised if they knew what I have done. They think me so kind and gentle. They know not what the whore has done to me. Maybe I should tell them. My brothers could offer me the solace I crave for my soul. My medicine keeps me from ripping more whores wide though I do not know how long I can remain calm. I am having to take more to still my mind but the pain is sometimes too much to bear.

So where to begin again I cannot decide. The city of whores seems a good place. But not yet. It is still too soon. The fools across the ocean still discuss me. I see mention of my deeds in the newspaper. They still marvel at my work after all this time – ha ha. The next time will be better. I will create something that no one will ever be able to diminish. My thrills call out to me thrilling thrilling. Their souls must tear apart their bodies rip open like ripe fruit. I will taste them – perhaps I shall take some and cook it for tea. Not long Sir Jim not long. Soon they will know your name. The others were just to warm up. I have something better in mind for the city of whores.

Whore Whore Whore

She teases me. I believe she knows about mine. She says little but her face smirks at me. Let the whoremaster have her. Bobo settles my mind but soon I must be working once again. The whore can keep her little secrets as I do mine. She knows not of Sir Jim and his deeds done and yet to come. Where once I had only love in my heart for her I now have only blackness.

Whore Whore Whore

I read they suspected that fool quack Tumbelty for my work in Austin. He was too busy exposing himself to other men to carry out my deeds. I know the whore has another. A whoremaster he shall be. So be it. He will keep her busy and I can carry on. My dreams command I begin again. I already know where but not yet. It is still to soon. I must wait. When I begin again it will be perfect. It will be something never forgotten. I will treat them to my very finest work indeed.

My darling Gladys lightens my dark soul. I had hoped she would mend the distance between Florie and I. The whoremaster can keep her and I will keep mine. Damn her for making me seek solace with another. Damn her for making me kill those whores. Damn her, damn her, damn her.

I need to be working again. I know now where and I know now when. They call themselves the Brethren. A populous set of fools who think I can help them with their sycophantic cause. I will consider it. But not yet. The whores of the city will fear my undertaking. It will be the perfect joke. Too subtle for the fools to work it out I imagine. It matters not. Once I have begun again what I achieve will be talked about the world around. Oh yes they will remember Sir Jim and his whores.

Jack be nimble Jack with his blade Jack left the whore bloody and flayed

The bitch thinks we need a nanny for Bobo and Gladys. I have left her to it. As long as it does not interfere with my plans then I care not. Michael and Edwin came to see me today. They thought I looked pale. I feel stronger than ever but must admit sometimes the pain is so great it is all I can do to not cry out in the night. My medicine still works but more and more of it I am needing. I sometimes wonder if the pain it causes is worth the pain it settles. But I will need it once I start again. It will keep me strong and calm my mind.

George asked about the bitch and the children in the club. The people went about their business unaware of who was in their midst. What would they think if they knew. It makes me smile to know that I am so very clever ha ha. They are talking to the man who tore those women wide in Austin and smile at me as though they wish to be my lover. I wonder how much they would be smiling as I cut into them and pulled out their intestines and placed them on their shoulders. Perhaps I will do that with one of them when I begin again. I think I would like to cut the breasts off one too. Yes that would be perfect.

The time is drawing near. I need to begin my campaign again soon. Battlecrease is slowly becoming home. Bunny and the children are happier here than at Grassendale. I had not the heart to start again so soon no heart – ha ha. When I begin the world will know of me and my work on the whores. London still calls to me but perhaps Manchester would be better. Closer to home and to the whore and her whoremaster.

Last night was the most difficult yet. How I stopped from squeezing the life from her I know not. She taunts me with her looks and movements. I need to begin again soon or else I fear what will become of me. My medicine helps somewhat but I am needing to take more and more to dull the pain. Writing is all that keeps me from being out there tonight. The whores stay safe because I sit here writing.

My pen it keeps my hands from killing They walk the streets with charm
 It keeps them safe from harm
 Sir Jack Jim will see them soon he thinks And watch their guts all spilling

Those fools contacted me again today. They wish
to control me. My campaign will not bow down to
the whims of a group of incompetent idiots. Yet
afterwards I wondered if I was too hasty. They have
power and could help me find women whores who
would not be missed. They could help with the
police fools though they are. Perhaps I should give
it some thought tonight. I will take my medicine
and think on their offer once more.

I met with their man Duggan today. A simple
lackey. I insisted that next time I meet the man in
charge. They say they know of Austin. They think I
am a fool and that they can blackmail me. But I
know what they need. I knew the whores were put
on this earth for a reason. Perhaps my campaign
has a higher meaning. I will slit him from ear to ear
should he mention Austin the next time we meet.
Meet again we shall. The brethren want Sir Jim
they shall have him. Let the streets run red with the
whores blood and know my campaign is believed in
by others.

I cannot sleep. My dreams are fraught with Bunny
and the children. Dear god what am I becoming to
think they can stay safe if I continue on this path.
She cuts at my soul yet I cannot let her go. My
darling Bunny you will be the death of me. Love is
tearing my soul apart.

Sir Jim will see them bleed Sir Jim will satisfy
their need

I cannot bear it any longer. I must begin my

campaign soon otherwise I fear what may happen to me. The children lift my mood but I know it will not last. It has been too long. I am needing more – more medicine more whores to rip. Austin now seems so far. I must decide soon where I am to begin again but the courage eludes me. Dear god what have I become.

The bitch thinks I am stupid. I know she sees him when I am away. I have no proof she sees him with the children. How he will suffer if he has been near my children. Perhaps I should begin with him – how that would confuse them. I have not done a man since Austin. He brought less pleasure but tore just the same. Perhaps the whoremaster will be better.

I feel lost and cold. My hands are always cold as I think is my heart. My dear Bunny see what you have done to me. I have been driven to this madness. More and more medicine I am taking to remain in control but I fear it will not be long before I will be upon the whores to have what I need. The thought of such pleasures thrills me like never before. Michael and Edwin must never know. They think me a gentle man. I hope Bunny and the children will remember me as the same.

I met with Duggan again today. He told me that his employer wishes to meet with me. Very well. I shall play their little game. If it brings me closer to my work beginning anew then I shall dance with them. They have more to lose than I should any of this become known. I have faith they will keep my secret as I will keep theirs.

I am confused as to whether I should end it all. I am taking more medicine to dull the pain. What would become of my family should my writing be discovered? It would destroy Michael and Edwin. The so-called Brethren have told me it matters not when I start again and that it is up to me. I do not know if I am able to go on. I have dreams of the women I have killed. I know I will be made to suffer for what I have done.

My thoughts are clear today. I was foolish thinking I should stop. The whores need to suffer. I walked the streets today amongst the pathetic people who think they are important. They know not of what I am capable of and what I will achieve. I have decided for now to accept their support. They have a great deal of power that can be used to allow my work to continue uninterrupted. They think they can control me. The Brethren and the whores. If they knew what they have in store for them they would stop this instant. But do I desire that? My answer is no. They will suffer just as I. I will see to that. Received a letter from Michael perhaps I will visit him. Will have to come to some sort of decision regards the children. I long for peace of mind but I sincerely believe that that will not come until I have sought my revenge on the whore and the whoremaster.

AFTERWORD

The Diary of Jack the Ripper announced its presence to
the world in 1992 via the hands of Michael Barrett, his
wife Anne Barrett nee Graham and Tony Devereux, in the
guise of a journal allegedly written by Liverpool cotton
merchant, James Maybrick.

This journal, though providing no name directly, gave
enough clues and references for Maybrick's identity to be
established.

Alongside a watch presented in 1993 by Albert Johnson
housing initials which seemed to corroborate the journal's
claims, the life of James Maybrick suddenly became of
interest to the planet and every Ripperologist and
armchair criminologist living upon it. With James
Maybrick's identity came that of his wife, Florence.

Prior to the discovery of the journal, James Maybrick's
name was ironically already noted in history for a very
different reason – death from arsenic overdose. Florence
was charged and sentenced for his murder, a sentence later
overturned by Queen Victoria herself after strong public

pressure that her trial had been a miscarriage of justice, a belief many historians share.

I deliberately chose to start this story at the end of the Ripper murders, as they had been written about and described so many times before by better authors than I. Instead, I wanted to use them and Jack the Ripper's legacy as a springboard for a conspiracy story that could not only act as a standalone story, but as a prequel to its companion story, Hellbound.

When discovered, the journal had pages missing from the front as though torn out. I used this opportunity to theorise (in a fictional way as authors do) the details they may have held about Maybrick's state of mind and other crimes he is suspected of being involved in prior to Whitechapel.

I have merged the fictional entries into the beginning of the actual journal so that they might form one elucidation of a man's journey into madness. I am not trying to convince you of whether James Maybrick was Jack the Ripper – that is only my opinion and one interpretation of the wealth of facts and details out there regarding the Whitechapel murderer. I just find it the most fascinating and therefore used it as a starting point for this tale.

Though I have taken artistic license with some of the events and pretty much every conversation, nearly all of the characters, their situations and fates are factually accurate as far as my research allowed. The Austin Murders were real, Florence Maybrick's fate was real, Thomas Quinn's fate was real, The Brethren are fictional, but their insidious schemes have some basis in historical fact.

If you enjoy this tale of historical, albeit fictional, intrigue, please check out Shirley Harrison's The Diary of

Jack the Ripper and The Diary of Jack the Ripper; The American Connection, Paul Feldman's Jack the Ripper; The Final Chapter, Did She Kill Him by Kate Colquhoun and Mrs Maybrick's Own Story; My Fifteen Lost Years by Florence Elizabeth Chandler Maybrick.

Any mistakes are my own.

ABOUT THE AUTHOR

David on the living room set from Sherlock.
Benedict Cumberbatch not included.

David McCaffrey was born in Middlesbrough, raised in
West Sussex and now lives in Redcar. He worked in the
NHS for many years, his last position being Lead Nurse in
Infection Prevention and Control at James Cook
University Hospital.
He started writing following the birth of his first son and in
2010 was accepted onto the writing coach programme run
by Steve Alten, international bestselling author of *Meg* and
The Mayan Prophecy. *Hellbound* was the result and the rest, as
they say, is history (cliche, cliche).
Though psychological thrillers are his *raison d'etre*, David is
also an activist for bullying and harassment in the NHS.
His book, 'Do No Harm: Bullying and Harassment in the

NHS' went to Number One in the Nursing and White Collar Crime categories of Amazon Kindle charts in November 2018 and was the Number One bestselling book in the U.S Amazon Kindle charts for more than three weeks in the Issues, Trends and Roles category.

David is a proud supporter and donator to the Ben Cohen StandUp Foundation which tackles bullying across the board, from schools to the workplace. He had the honour of being invited to speak at the Standup Foundation's Inaugural Conference in November 2018.

Half of all profits from 'Do No Harm' go to the Ben Cohen Foundation.

David lives with his wife Kelly, has a Jakey, a Liam (a.k.a Gruffy) and a Cole (a.k.a Baby Moo Man) They also have an Obi... who's the dog.

facebook.com/www.davidmccaffrey.net

twitter.com/daveymac1975

instagram.com/mccaffreydavid

ALSO BY DAVID MCCAFFREY

Hellbound (Book One in the Hellbound Anthology)

Nameless (Book Three in the Hellbound Anthology)

The Warmest Place to Hide

Do No Harm: Bullying and Harassment in the NHS

By Any Means Necessary (ghost writer) by Stephen Sayers

.